Where Did All the Dragons Go?

Where Did All the Dragons Go?

by Fay Robinson

illustrated by Victor Lee

BridgeWater Books

Library of Congress Cataloging-in-Publication Data
Robinson, Fay.
Where did all the dragons go? / by Fay Robinson ; pictures by Victor Lee.
p.   cm.
Summary: Ever since the dragon leader boomed "Now's the time,"
all the dragons flew away, leaving children to wonder
where they went but also believing they still live.
ISBN 0-8167-3808-4
[1. Dragons—Fiction. 2. Stories in rhyme.]   I. Lee, Victor, ill.   II. Title.
PZ8.3.R57Wh   1996   [E]—dc20   95-3620

For Carl. —F.R.

Dedicated to Hanako for her patience and for being there. Special thanks to Mum and Dad. —V.L.

Long ago and by and by,
dragons ruled the earth and sky.

They scaled the mountains,
climbed the trees,
slept in castles,
swam the seas,

and flew; they FLEW the turquoise skies
with gilded wings and amber eyes.

Some with feathers, some with scales,
some with furry heads and tails.
Gentle dragons, young and old,
hoarding gemstones, guarding gold,
gathering in dragon crowds,
breathing fire, making clouds.

The fiery games that dragons played
made men and women quite afraid.

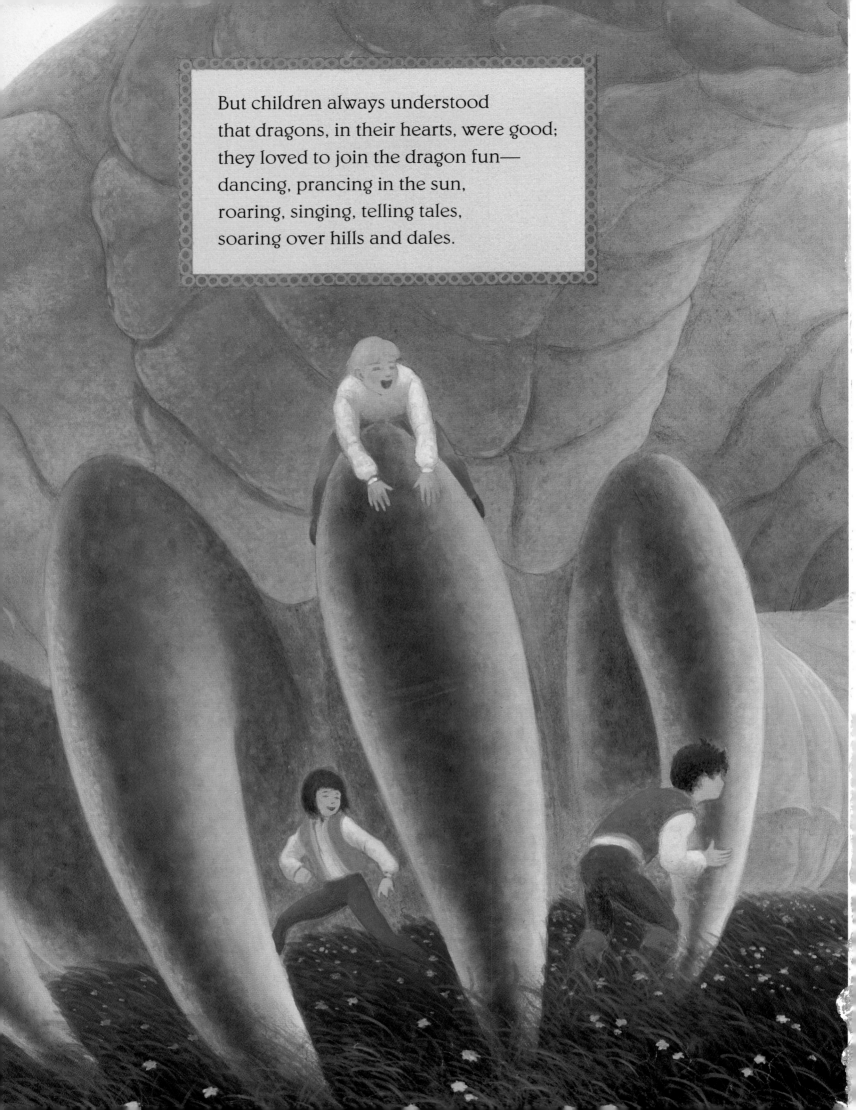

But children always understood
that dragons, in their hearts, were good;
they loved to join the dragon fun—
dancing, prancing in the sun,
roaring, singing, telling tales,
soaring over hills and dales.

Then one starry autumn night,
the dragons woke up with a fright.
Their leader's voice boomed overhead—
"Now's the time" was all it said.

Little dragons, big ones too,
every one knew what to do.

Those on mountains,
those in trees,
those in castles,
those in seas,
all let out a dragon sigh,
all took wing and filled the sky.

Children heard a thunderous sound
as dragon wings beat all around.
From every home across the land,
children scurried hand in hand
and watched those dragons flying by,
watched and sadly wondered why.

Sparks, like lightning, lit the way.
Dragons slowly flew away—
over mountains,
over trees,
over castles,
over seas—

then,
at the edge of earth and sky,
dragons called a sad good-bye.

That's the last 'twas ever heard
of dragons—not another word.

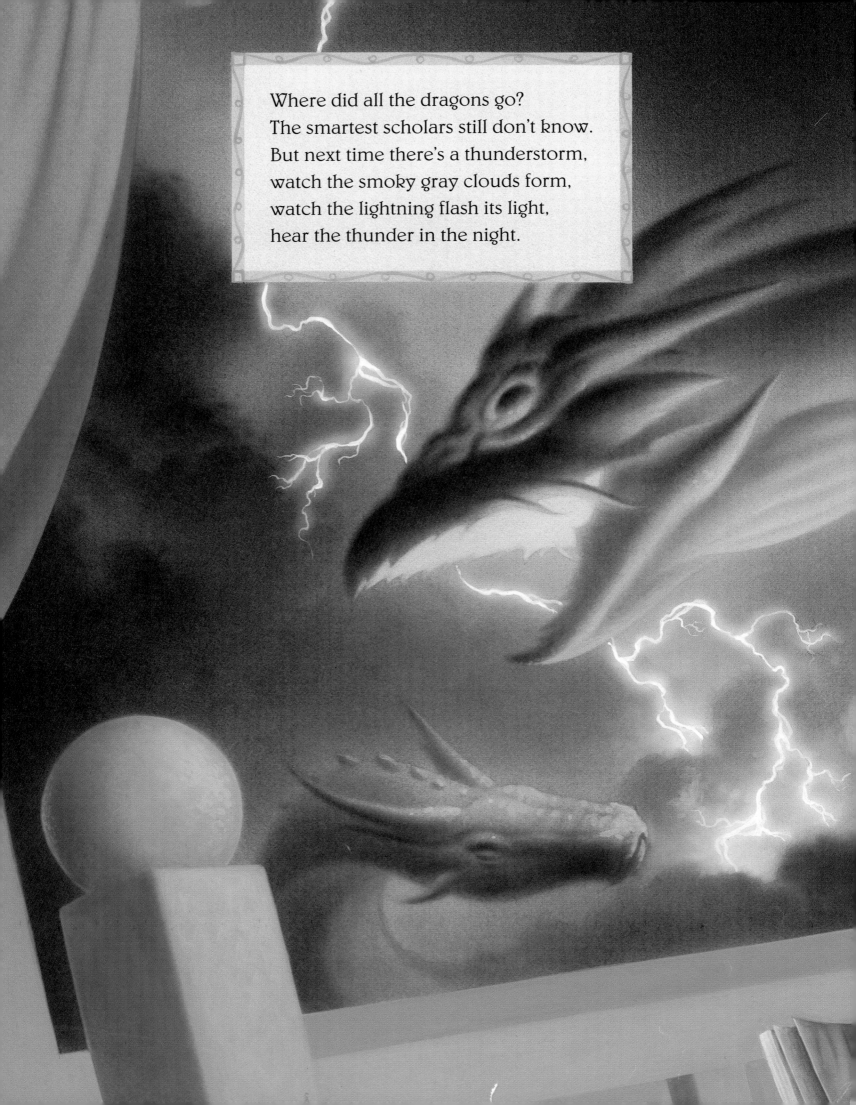

Where did all the dragons go?
The smartest scholars still don't know.
But next time there's a thunderstorm,
watch the smoky gray clouds form,
watch the lightning flash its light,
hear the thunder in the night.

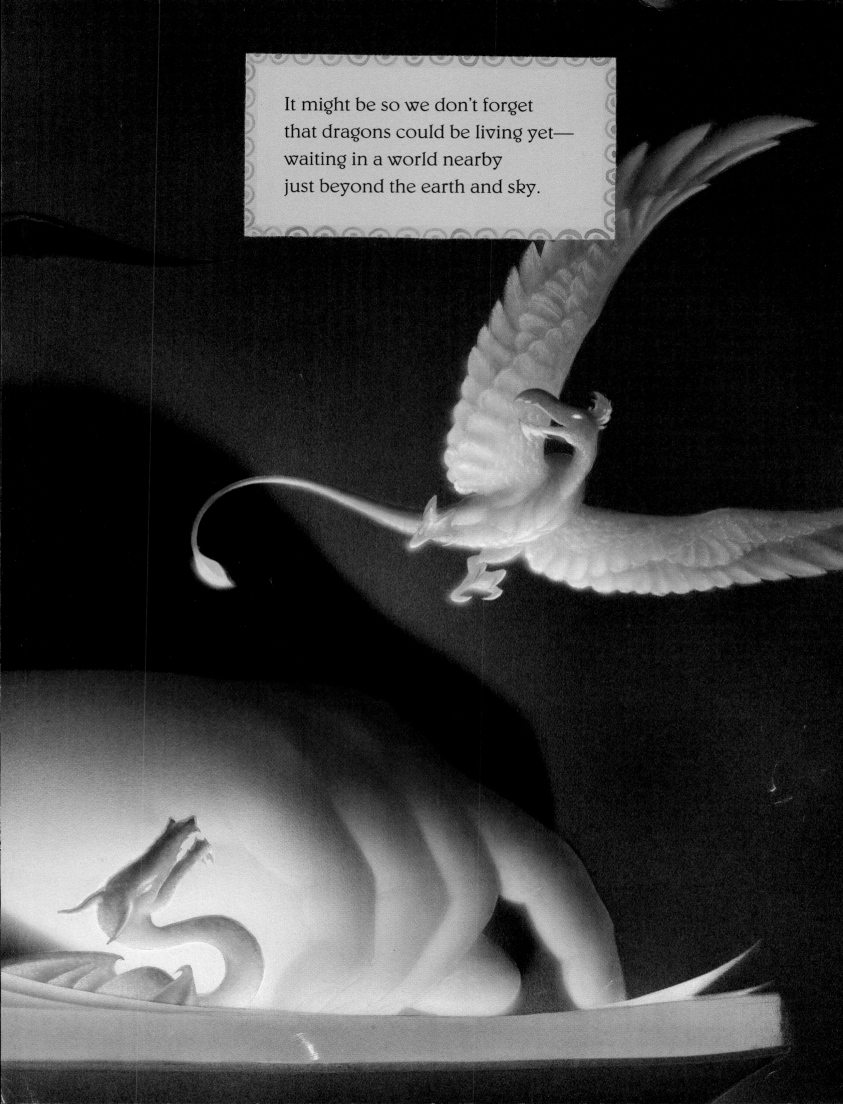

It might be so we don't forget
that dragons could be living yet—
waiting in a world nearby
just beyond the earth and sky.